EINSTEIN ANDERSON
Science Detective

THE ON-LINE SPACEMAN

AND OTHER CASES

by Seymour Simon

illustrated by S.D. Schindler

Morrow Junior Books
NEW YORK

To Benjamin, Chloe, and Joel,
with love

Printed in the United States of America.

2   3   4   5   6   7   8   9   10

Library of Congress Cataloging-in-Publication Data
Simon, Seymour.
The on-line spaceman and other cases/by Seymour Simon.
    p. cm.—(Einstein Anderson, science detective)
Summary: Einstein Anderson uses his scientific knowledge to solve a variety
of problems, from crying rocks to a backward monster.
                ISBN 0-688-14433-0
[1. Science—Problems, exercises, etc.—Fiction.]   I. Title.   II. Series: Simon,
Seymour. Einstein Anderson, science detective.
PZ7.S60573On 1997 [Fic]—dc20   96-34416   CIP AC

CONTENTS

1

The Case of the

ON-LINE

SPACEMAN

It certainly doesn't feel like early autumn!"
Einstein Anderson muttered to himself
as he hurried down the dark road that
led to Stanley's house. Einstein shivered as a
cold September wind pushed against him.
The shadowy tree branches whipped back and
forth against one another, making strange
crying sounds. The moon struggled to shine
through the dark clouds overhead. Autumn
had begun only a few days ago, but there was
a chill in the air and a hint of snow in the
clouds.

If he walked fast, Einstein could get to Stanley's house in ten minutes. But most times it took him at least an hour, because he usually stopped to look at leaves, ants, spiders, birds, rotting logs, stars, and anything else that caught his eye. But tonight Einstein was in a hurry. Stanley had mentioned something about a strange thing that had happened and had asked Einstein to come over as quickly as he could.

Einstein Anderson was in sixth grade. He was thin, a bit taller than average height, and had dark hair. The eyeglasses he wore always seemed a bit too big for his face, and he was forever pushing them back when they slid down his nose. His brown eyes often had a faraway look, as if he were thinking about some interesting science experiment. But Einstein was not always serious. In fact, he loved a good joke—and even a bad one—and liked to make puns...the worse, the better.

Einstein's real name was Adam. But few people called him that anymore. Adam had been interested in science and nature since he had learned how to talk. By the time he went to school, he could solve science mysteries that stumped even his teachers.

At the age of six, he had shared his knowledge about science with Ms. Moore, his kindergarten teacher. She was so impressed that she had given him the nickname of Einstein, after Albert Einstein, the most famous scientist of the twentieth century. Eventually, all his friends—and sometimes even his parents—called him Einstein.

By the time Einstein arrived at Stanley's house, he was breathing hard. He pressed the doorbell, and a strange voice boomed from behind the door. "Friend or foe?"

"It's me." Einstein's voice quavered a bit. That doesn't sound like Stanley. What in the world is going on? he thought.

"Friend or foe? Friend or foe? Friend or ggggrrrr..." The voice growled to a stop, and the door was flung open. A dark figure appeared at the entrance. Einstein had a small moment of panic before he recognized his friend.

"That dumb recording I made should stop after one announcement," Stanley complained. "I can't figure out why it keeps repeating itself." Stanley motioned Einstein to come in. "Why do you look so strange? And how come it took you so long to get here?" he asked impatiently.

"The journey, not the arrival, matters." Einstein smiled. "If you want to see time fly, throw your clock out the window."

Stanley groaned. He brushed his long black hair away from his face. "Stop telling me those corny jokes," he said. "This is serious. I think I have made an incredible discovery. I think I am in contact with an ET, an extraterrestrial. An encounter of the third

4

kind. A lonely visitor from outer space. I'm usually very skeptical about space monsters, but this time I know it's true. Come on up to my laboratory, and I'll show you."

"You know why monster families stay together for so long? Because they can't stand to kiss each other good-bye," Einstein joked as he followed his friend upstairs. Stanley groaned again.

Stanley Roberts was a junior at Sparta Senior High School. Despite their age difference, Einstein and Stanley were good friends. Stanley was very interested in science and often invited Einstein to come over to his house to see his inventions and experiments.

Stanley pushed open the door to his "laboratory." It was really an attic room that his mom and dad had permitted him to use for his experiments. The room was a complete mess, as usual. Several computers hummed, their displays flickering in changing colors. Bunsen burners, glass test tubes, half-finished experiments, and strange-looking contraptions were everywhere. It looked like a junk shop, but Stanley insisted that it was all scientific apparatus.

"This is something really big-time," said Stanley. "An alien race will be able to tell me all kinds of things that no one on Earth knows. I'll become famous. And I'll build a great big laboratory, where I can do all kinds of neat experiments." He paused. "Einstein, my friend," Stanley continued, "I want you to help me contact this space visitor and share in my glory."

"Help you? How?" Einstein asked cautiously. He had the feeling that Stanley was setting him up to do something silly. He adjusted his glasses, and they promptly slid down again to the end of his nose. He pushed them back with one finger and said, "Are you sure this alien is real? The last time you asked me to help you with something like this, it turned out to be a phony baby Loch Ness monster."

"Forget about that," Stanley said impatiently. "This is something completely different. I have absolute proof. I got it from a new website I found on the Internet."

"New websites? Isn't that what you call two spiders who just got married? Newly webs?" Einstein asked with an innocent smile. He knew that a website was a location on the worldwide telephone network called the Internet. Websites usually displayed text and graphics and sometimes even sound and motion pictures. Einstein had used computer code to construct his own website, on which he posted all kinds of interesting experiments and new discoveries in science.

"Your website is not the only science on the Internet," Stanley said, ignoring Einstein's joke. "About a week ago, I was surfing the Internet, looking for new science experiments to do, when I came upon this strange website. Here, let me show you."

Stanley sat down in front of one of his computers. His fingers flew across the keyboard as he connected to the Internet through the modem. The screen lit up with flashing red words spread against a background of twinkling stars. The words read: *Help! I am from a moon circling a planet that Earth astronomers call 70 Virginis B. My space-*

ship has crash-landed on your planet. Please contact me. I need your assistance to return to my home planet.

"That's very interesting," said Einstein. "I read about the discovery of some new planets beyond the solar system. The first planetary system beyond our own was discovered in the early 1990s. Since then, a number of other planets have been discovered, including one called 70 Virginis B."

"What do we know about that planet?" asked Stanley. "Is it possible that life could come from there?"

"It's possible," replied Einstein cautiously. "The star, 70 Virginis, is very much like our sun. The planet discovered circling it is about eight times the mass of Jupiter. Temperatures on the planet, or on any moons it might have, could possibly support life. In fact, some astronomers call the planet Goldilocks, because the temperature is 'just right' for liquid water to exist. But just because the so-called alien says he comes from there doesn't mean that he does."

"Don't you think I know that?" Stanley said, brushing back his black hair, which kept falling across his face. "But I wrote to the e-mail address on the website, asking for some proof, and got a reply along with a computer file containing a scan of a photograph. Here, let me show it to you."

Stanley typed something on the keyboard, and a photo of a strange blue being appeared on the computer screen. Behind the blue creature was a weird-looking building. The blue figure certainly looked peculiar. Einstein bent down and peered at the screen more closely. The creature seemed to be holding up a placard that had some words written on it. "What do those words say?" Einstein asked.

"I couldn't make them out, either," said Stanley. "So I asked the alien to send me the original photo. It came in the mail today. Here it is. And here's the letter that came along with it. This creature—he calls himself a Klaatu—needs money to buy parts for his spaceship. He says that if I send him one hundred dollars, he will send me a scientific discovery that will make me famous. But the photo is blurry, and I still can't read the words on that sign that he's carrying. They seem to be in some kind of strange language."

Einstein picked up the photo and looked at it thoughtfully. "You know, Stanley, this photo might be a fake. This creature does look very strange, but for all we know, it could be a person in a pair of blue pajamas and a mask. Nowadays, it's easy to fake a photo on a computer, and no one can tell whether it's real or not. In fact, many of the special effects in movies are put together on a computer. I'm not sure if there's any way you can prove it's real."

Einstein took out the magnifying lens that he carried with him and studied the photo. Then he looked at the same photo on the screen. He typed in several commands, and the photo became clearer. Then he played with the image, changing the colors and then reversing the photo, left to right. Suddenly his face broke into a huge smile, and he started to laugh. "I guess I can prove that this photo is a fake, after all," he said. He walked over to a mirror and held the photo in front of him. "Look at this, Stanley," he said.

"All I can see is your face in the mirror, grinning from ear to ear," said Stanley. "What am I supposed to be looking at?"

"Look at the writing on the sign," said Einstein. "This is just a hoax to get you to send money. I first saw it on the computer, but the mirror also lets you see what the sign says."

Can you solve the mystery: How can a mirror help Einstein read the words on the "alien's" sign?

"I still don't see what you're talking about," said Stanley. "And what can a mirror show that I can't see just by looking at something?"

"A mirror does something very interesting," explained Einstein. "As you know, it reverses images from left to right. So if you write something on a piece of paper and look at it in a mirror, the writing looks backward."

"So what?" asked Stanley.

"Well, if you write something backward and then look at it in a mirror, it now appears the right way, and you can read it. So just read what is written on the sign this blue meanie is holding."

Stanley looked at the mirror image of the writing. Now he could make out what the words were: JOE'S DINER HAS MONSTROUSLY GOOD FOOD.

Stanley groaned and shook his head. "How could I have believed in that dumb picture? Just let me get to my computer and write a letter to that blue spaceman!"

"Wait a minute." Einstein laughed. "If a spaceman is that blue, shouldn't you just try to cheer him up?"

2

The Case of the

FAR-OUT FRISBEE

Move the sign higher and to the right." Margaret waved her hand at Einstein. Einstein was standing on a tall ladder. He was holding a large cardboard placard that read: LUNAR OLYMPICS YEAR 2100 AT MOON BASE I. "The sign should be centered at the top of the bulletin board," Margaret added.

Einstein sighed. "This ladder is kind of rickety," he complained. He moved the sign a bit to the right. "How's this?" he asked.

"You moved the sign too much," said

Margaret. "Move it a little over to the left now and a little farther down." She paused while Einstein adjusted the sign. "Yes," she said, "that's good. You can tack it into place."

Einstein started to hammer small tacks to hold the sign in place. "Ouch!" he yelled. "I just hit my thumb with the hammer." He

looked down at Margaret. "You know, I just thought of how to hammer a tack without hitting my thumb."

"How are you going to do that?" asked Margaret.

"I'm going to let you hold the tack," replied Einstein with a grin.

Margaret tried to stop from smiling at Einstein's joke. Margaret Michaels was Einstein's best friend in school. She was also his rival. Science was their favorite subject. Einstein and Margaret had been good friends since second grade, when Margaret had brought in her rock collection and Einstein had helped her identify some of the different minerals in the rocks. Since then, they were always talking about important things like the new dinosaur discoveries, how to program their computers, and who was the best science student.

Margaret's mother was proud of her daughter but a little bewildered by her. Mrs. Michaels had wanted Margaret to take ballet and piano lessons after school. Margaret had insisted on spending after-school time at the school science club, along with Einstein.

Mrs. Michaels thought that animals were nice when they were outside her house. Margaret thought that animals were nice both outside and inside the house. She had a pet springer spaniel named Nova, cats named Orville and Wilbur, an ant farm, a jar full of worms, a snake named Pat (named after the class bully), and a pet gerbil named Sammy.

Margaret had just adopted two kittens that had been born in her backyard. She named one Mittens, because of his white paws. She named the other one Sir Isaac Newton, after the great scientist who lived three hundred years ago and discovered the laws of gravity and motion. Sir Isaac Newton (the kitten) was always running around and sticking his nose into everything. Margaret often had to call out to stop the kitten from climbing on her science experiments. It was difficult to say "Sir Isaac Newton" quickly. So Margaret began to call the cat Newty, or sometimes Newty Frewty.

Margaret and Einstein had gotten permission to stage a mock Lunar Olympics in their school in order to raise money for a telescope for the after-school space and astronomy club. They were now in the process of thinking up the details of all kinds of events and contests that might take place on the moon.

"The moon's gravity is only one-sixth that of Earth's," Einstein pointed out, "so a person will weigh only one-sixth as much on the moon. And he or she also can jump higher and farther and pick up heavier weights." He thought for a second and then asked, "Do you know which is heavier, Margaret, a full moon or a quarter moon?"

"The moon weighs the same all month long," said Margaret, puzzled. "Why should one phase be heavier than another?"

"Because a full moon is lighter than a quarter moon," explained Einstein with a smile. "Lighter, get it?"

Margaret groaned. She liked Einstein's jokes—usually, anyway—but was determined not to tell him that. "The difference in gravity between the moon and the Earth should give us lots of ideas about what to do," said

Margaret. "We can make a lunar scale to show how much you weigh on the moon by changing the numbers. We can also have a weight-lifting contest and all kinds of distance throwing contests. There can be a baseball-throwing contest and a Frisbee-tossing contest. Can you imagine how far a Frisbee will fly on the moon? Out of sight!"

"Well," agreed Einstein, "the weight-lifting and baseball-throwing contests will work just fine. But a Frisbee can fly farther on Earth than it can on the moon."

"That's silly, Einstein," said Margaret. "On the moon, a Frisbee will weigh only one-sixth as much as it weighs on Earth. Isn't that right?"

"Yup," agreed Einstein. He pushed his glasses back. "Still won't go as far," he said.

"Is that so?" said Margaret. "You can hit a golf ball farther on the moon. I remember reading that one of the Apollo astronauts, Alan Shepard, hit a couple of golf balls during his lunar landing back in 1971. He said that one ball he hit would have gone thirty yards on Earth, but because the moon has no atmosphere and so little gravity, the ball went about two hundred yards and landed in a crater."

"Would you call that a crater in one?" Einstein asked with a grin. He pushed back his glasses again.

"Enough jokes," responded Margaret. "If a golf ball goes more than six times as far, then a Frisbee will also go six times as far. It stands to reason!"

"Some things that seem to stand to reason don't," said Einstein. "The Earth looks mostly flat from where we stand, yet we know that the Earth is round. Does that make sense? Does it make sense that white is a mixture of all the colors of the rainbow? It may not seem to make sense, but a lunar Frisbee is just not going to go anywhere near as far as an Earth Frisbee. Making sense of something means finding out more about it than you already know."

Can you solve the mystery: Why is Einstein so sure that a Frisbee will fly farther on Earth than on the moon?

"Einstein, I think you're just a know-it-all," said Margaret. "Why do you *think* that a Frisbee won't fly as far on the moon?"

"Just a know-it-all who knows it all," replied Einstein with a smile. "Seriously," he continued, "when a Frisbee is thrown on Earth, air moves faster over the top of it than under the bottom, because of its shape. That creates a lower pressure on the top, so the pressure on the bottom is greater. The difference in air pressure keeps the Frisbee flying longer."

"I see," said Margaret thoughtfully. "Since there is no air on the moon, there is no lifting effect that air provides. This means that the distance a Frisbee would fly on the moon depends mostly on how hard it's thrown."

"Right," agreed Einstein. "The same kind of thing would happen if you had a paper-airplane-flying contest on the moon. It would just be a matter of how far you could throw the plane. The design of the plane would not make any important difference. A baseball would go farther on the moon than on Earth, because air only slows it down on Earth, and there is no air on the moon."

3

The Case of the

SPEEDY PASTA

It was a lovely cool autumn day in October, and Einstein was on his way to school. He stopped to admire the tree leaves, which ranged in color from yellow and gold to bronze and fiery scarlet. Einstein knew that the autumn leaves were colored by two chemicals, one that produced the yellows and the other, the reds. He also knew that these colors had been in the leaves even during the summer, but that they had been hidden by the bright green of chlorophyll. Now that the days were growing shorter, the leaves were producing less chlorophyll. And with less green, the other colors could be seen.

Einstein had just bent down to pick up a beautiful yellow leaf from the ground when he felt himself being pushed from behind. He staggered forward and barely managed to keep from falling on his face. When he turned, he saw two of his least favorite classmates, Pat the Brat and his sidekick, Herman.

Pat was the biggest kid in Einstein's class. He was also the meanest. Everyone called him Pat the Brat. Only not to his face. His friend Herman was the second-meanest kid in the class. They were always picking on smaller kids.

"Oops, did I bump against you accidentally?" asked Pat with a nasty smile. "Next time watch out when you bend down. You never know what's coming up behind you."

"You do look like an accident waiting to happen, Pat," answered Einstein. He knew that he could fight Pat if he had to, but he would rather handle him by thinking.

"Huh?" said Herman.

"Shut up, Herman," said Pat. "Now listen to me, Einstein. The class cooking contest is this afternoon. The winner in each group will get free tickets to the circus that's coming to town. Now, you *know* that I want to win that contest. So I have a little bet to make with you. And I'm sure that you want to make the bet with me." Pat clenched his fists and looked at them carefully. "Do you understand what I mean?"

"Well, I'm sure you're speaking your own mind," said Einstein. "Which does limit the conversation," he added under his breath.

"What'd you say, Einstein?" asked Pat angrily.

"Yeah!" said Herman.

"I just said that this is an interesting conversation. But I don't know what you want to bet," said Einstein.

"Here's the way I see it," said Pat. "You and I are the only ones in the class who are going to make pasta. And that means that only *one* of us is going to win in the pasta group. Now, naturally, I expect to win, because I know that you are going to drop out of the contest."

"I'm not dropping out of the contest, Pat," replied Einstein warily. "Why should I?"

"That's the little bet that we are going to make," said Pat. "I knew you weren't just going to drop out because I asked you to. So I cooked up this bet about the cooking. Ha, ha. Get it? Cooked up about the cooking?"

"I get it," said Einstein. "You're just an old softy. With a head to match."

"Huh?" said Herman.

"Never mind my head, Einstein," said Pat.

"Here's the bet. You have to boil water to make pasta. So we're both going to start with the same amount of water in the same kind of pot on the same kind of stove. The person whose water boils first wins the bet, and the other person has to drop out of the contest. Now is that fair or is that fair?"

"It sounds silly to me," said Einstein. "What difference does it make whose water boils first? Why can't we just have the contest and see whose pasta tastes better?"

"Because I know that my water will boil first," said Pat. "My grandmother gave me all kinds of tips about cooking. And one of the tips is how to make water boil quickly. So, Mr. Einstein Smarty, that's the bet. And there is no way you are going to win."

"Let me get this straight," said Einstein. "The amount of water, the pot, and the heat of the stove are all going to be the same. If those are the conditions, then I'll go along with the bet."

"Good," said Pat. He punched Herman on the arm. "Let's get going."

"Huh?" said Herman.

Einstein shook his head. What could Pat be up to, he wondered. How could he be so sure that he was going to win? Could Pat actually know a secret that would make water boil faster?

Einstein continued on his way to school. It seemed to him that both pots of water should boil at the same time. But all during the morning, he wondered about how water could be made to boil faster. And as he went down to the lunchroom with his friend Margaret, Einstein had still not thought of a solution to the mystery.

"Why are you so worried, Einstein?" asked Margaret. "Pat has never won a contest with you before. Why should this time be any different?"

Einstein didn't answer. He and Margaret went through the lunch line and sat down at a table with their food.

"Don't look now, Einstein," said Margaret, "but Pat and Herman just came in and are sitting right behind us."

Einstein didn't turn around. He could hear Pat and Herman yelling and banging the table behind him. "You've heard the expression 'The worst is yet to come'? Well, it's just arrived," said Einstein.

"Well, look who's here," Pat suddenly exclaimed. "It's Einstein, the loser! You can't possibly win the bet."

"Yeah," said Herman. "We're going to add salt to the cooking water. And Pat's grandma told him that adding salt will make the water boil faster, so you're out."

"Shut up, Herman! Einstein just heard what you said, and he's going to add salt, too. But I'll just add more salt than him." Pat grabbed Herman by the arm. "Let's get out of here."

After Pat and Herman left, Margaret looked at Einstein. "Did you hear that? Now what are you going to do? If Pat adds more salt to the water than you do, he's going to win the bet. I can't believe this! You may lose to Pat for the first time!"

Einstein started to laugh. "Me lose to Pat? Never!"

Can you solve the mystery: How does Einstein know that Pat is not going to win the bet?

"But, Einstein," said Margaret, "I know that adding salt to water will cook the pasta faster. I read that in a cookbook. So what's to stop Pat from adding more salt than you do and winning the bet?"

"I know that a cookbook is a book with a lot of stirring chapters, but in this case it's not a recipe for winning," Einstein joked.

Margaret smiled and groaned. "Come on, Einstein," she said. "Stop the jokes and tell me how in the world you can win the bet."

Einstein pushed back his glasses, which were slipping down off his nose. "Pasta will get cooked sooner if you add salt to water," he said, "but that's because the salt raises the boiling temperature of the water so the water is hotter after you heat it. But it takes *longer* to get the salty water to begin to boil, because you have to heat it to that higher temperature."

"I get it," exclaimed Margaret. "The more salt Pat adds, the longer it will take for the water to boil. So now he's sure to lose the bet to you. I'm so glad. Pat was boasting to everyone that he is not only the strongest kid

28

in the class but that he's smarter than you. The other kids just try to hide when they see him coming."

"Well, every year Pat finishes last in the school's popularity contest. And the only reason he finishes that high is that he votes for himself!"

"You'll just have to excuse him." Margaret laughed. "This is the year that his age caught up with his IQ."

"No one is perfect," said Einstein. "Especially Pat."

4

The Case of the

CRYING
ROCKS

It was one of those cloudy gray mornings that makes a person want to stay in bed. Einstein had been drowsily listening to the rain falling against the windowpane when his younger brother, Dennis, came into the room.

"Are you awake, Einstein?" Dennis shouted. "It's raining hard. Why are you just lying there and not getting out of bed? How come you didn't wake me up? Today's a school day. You're supposed to wake me up on school days. Just like I have the job to wake you up on weekends."

Dennis was in third grade and was always asking Einstein to explain something in science to him. Usually Einstein was very patient with Dennis and answered all his questions. But he privately thought that sometimes Dennis could be a bit of a pest, especially on weekend mornings when he wanted to sleep late.

Einstein stretched and yawned. He threw the covers off and shivered as he got out of bed. "Today's forecast wasn't too accurate, Dennis," Einstein said as he walked into the bathroom to wash and to brush his teeth. "The forecaster predicted a sunny and warm morning. I think I should let him know that 'sunny and warm' has been dripping down my window all morning. His forecast should have been: partly sunny, partly rainy, partly accurate."

Einstein toweled his face dry and looked over at his brother. "So why are you up so early on a school day, Dennis? You usually sleep like a log during the week and are up with the robins on weekends and holidays." He continued with a smile, "You know, when you cross a robin with a parrot, it not only wakes you up early, but it tells you the time."

Dennis groaned. "No jokes before breakfast, please," he said. "Mom asked me to make sure you got up early today. She's going to interview some professor this afternoon and wants to speak to you about his claims." Mrs. Anderson was an editor and writer for the Sparta *Tribune,* one of the local newspapers.

"Tell Mom that I'll be down in a few minutes," Einstein said. "How about making me some toast? I feel just a bit hungry. A light breakfast should be enough: orange juice, some cereal, a couple of eggs, and toast. And a glass of milk to wash everything down. Unless, of course, Mom or Dad wants to make pancakes. Then you can leave off the toast."

"I'm glad you're not really hungry," mumbled Dennis as he left Einstein and began going downstairs. "We'd need at least three hours to eat breakfast."

Einstein quickly got dressed in his favorite pair of jeans, which were getting a bit raggedy at the knees. He also put on a warm sweatshirt that said *Sparta Panthers* in purple across the front and a pair of beat-up sneakers.

When Einstein came down to the kitchen, Dennis was setting the table and Mrs. Anderson was pouring orange juice into glasses. Dr. Anderson was making scrambled eggs. He was a veterinarian, and sometimes he had to go out early on emergency calls at farms in the countryside before his sons got up in the morning. He grinned at Einstein and said, "Good morning. I see you've discovered a new use for old jeans. You wear them!"

"Well, I have a pair of jeans for every day of the year," Einstein replied. "And this pair is it."

His father groaned. Einstein loved to hear people groan after he cracked a joke. It meant they really understood it.

After breakfast, Einstein and his mother went into her study to talk. "I'm interested in what you think about Professor Witz," Mrs. Anderson said. "He's having a meeting this afternoon where he'll demonstrate his technique for getting water from rocks. He claims towns in the desert will be able to have a supply of water whenever they need it—and he's trying to get people to invest money with him. I thought you'd be playing baseball after school, but since it's raining, how about coming to the meeting with me?"

"Sure," agreed Einstein. "Sounds interesting. Though I can't imagine how you could get water from a stone. But I'd be happy to watch what the professor does and tell you what I think.

"Say," he added, "I just thought of something. If the formula for water is H_2O, is the formula for an ice cube H_2O squared?"

Mrs. Anderson chuckled. "I'll meet you at the Sparta Auditorium at four o'clock, just before Professor Witz's demonstration. Try not to be late."

Einstein arrived at the auditorium a few minutes before four. It was still cloudy and drizzly, and his jacket was wet all the way through. He saw his mother waiting near the entrance, and they hurried inside. "I thought you said you could wear your baseball jacket in the rain," she said.

"You can wear it," replied Einstein. "It just gets soaked."

"Take off that wet jacket," said Mrs. Anderson. "I'm not amused." She motioned to the stage. "I see Professor Witz is about to begin his demonstration. Let's see what's happening."

Onstage there was a table and several rocks. The rocks seemed to be covered with clumps of glassy white crystals. There was also a propane blowtorch and a pair of tongs. A video camera stood on a stand nearby, and two large television monitors were on either side of the table.

About twenty people were in the audience. The lights in the auditorium dimmed, and a man came onstage. He had a pair of protective goggles on top of his head and wore a long lab coat. His outfit reminded Einstein of the Halloween costume his brother, Dennis, wore trick-or-treating the previous week.

"Good afternoon," the man said in a deep voice. "I am Professor Witz. I have set up this demonstration to prove once and for all that I can get water from rocks. This great feat will allow people who live in the desert to get water whenever they need it. I am developing this process now. If you buy shares in my company, who knows what they will be worth in the future. Farsighted people who invested in computer companies a few years ago have made millions of dollars, even billions. Investing in making water from rocks might make you even more money in the future."

Professor Witz strode over to the table, pulling his goggles down over his eyes. He picked up the blowtorch and lit the flame. "Watch closely on the monitor screen," he said. "I will now make these rocks cry!"

The professor picked up one of the rocks with a pair of tongs and held it in the flame. On the monitor screen, it was plain to see that the crystals quickly began to bubble and boil, dripping down liquid. "Does anyone doubt that I have gotten water from rocks?" asked the professor. "You can see it with your own eyes. I will meet with all interested parties in the back of the auditorium and explain how you can invest in my company."

"Did you see that, Einstein?" asked Mrs. Anderson. "Should we meet with the professor? Has he really produced water from those rocks?"

"Let's go up to the stage and take a closer look," said Einstein. They walked up to the table, and Einstein peered down.

"Those really are rocks, and that really is water," said Einstein. "But anyone who gives him any money is just going to lose it faster than those rocks gave up water."

Can you solve the mystery: How does Einstein know that Professor Witz's plans to produce water from rocks are not worth anything as an investment?

"I don't understand," said Mrs. Anderson. "If that is really water coming from those rocks, shouldn't that be a valuable discovery for communities without water?"

"It might be, if the water came from common rocks that are found in a desert or from sand," said Einstein. "But Professor Witz didn't use ordinary rocks. He used a mineral called a zeolite. There have been only about thirty or so zeolites found in nature, and many others have been made in laboratories. Zeolites have many microscopic water-filled channels, and they appear to boil when you heat them. In fact, their name comes from Greek words that mean 'boiling stones.'"

"Still," said Mrs. Anderson, "couldn't communities use zeolites to keep producing water?"

"Once water leaves a zeolite," Einstein explained, "it has to be replaced in order for you to get more water from it. But if you are going to add water to the zeolite, you might as well just use the water in any other way that you need."

"Hmm!" exclaimed Mrs. Anderson, smiling at her son. "Professor Witz should have known better than to try to fool Einstein Anderson."

5

The Case of the

FEARLESS EXPLORER

 s. Warren, Einstein's social studies teacher, was reading to the class from an old leather-bound book.

"At the bottom of the world lies an unknown continent, still trapped in the Ice Age. This mighty continent is crisscrossed by enormous mountain ranges that no one has ever seen. In some places, the ice on the ground is more than two miles thick. Centered at the South Pole, this ice-covered land is almost as large as Europe and Australia combined. The continent is surrounded by the stormy waters of the Atlantic, the Pacific, and the Indian oceans. This is the place that I, Helmut Jorgansen, will fearlessly explore and conquer.

"Isn't that exciting, class? We've read about all kinds of explorers and discoveries, from Marco Polo to Ferdinand Magellan, from the voyages of Captain James Cook to the explorations of Lewis and Clark. Now that we are back from the Thanksgiving holiday, we are going to read an actual explorer's journal—a journal that was written more than one hundred years ago and was just found in the attic of a neighbor of mine. We may be one of the first classes that has ever read Jorgansen's writings.

"Now, who can tell me the name of the continent that Jorgansen writes about?"

Most of the students in the class raised their hands to answer the question. Even Pat and Herman had their hands up. Ms. Warren looked surprised at that.

"I'm glad to see that so many of you know the answer," she said. "Herman, why don't you tell us the name of the continent at the bottom of the world."

"Huh?" said Herman. "Could I change my seat, Ms. Warren? Someone is throwing spitballs at my head, and I can't think."

"Somehow that doesn't surprise me Herman," said Ms. Warren. "Pat, you tell us the answer."

"I have to go to the rest room, Ms. Warren," responded Pat.

"Not now," exclaimed the teacher. Her face was getting red. "Just answer the question."

"Sure, Herman can change his seat," replied Pat. "Now can I go?"

"Not Herman's question!" Ms. Warren's face was getting redder and redder. "The name of the icy continent around the South Pole. Like the Arctic, only down below. Now, what is it?"

"The Arctic—isn't that what that guy built when the floods came?" said Pat with a frown on his face. He looked over at Herman and winked.

"What?" exclaimed Ms. Warren. "What are you talking about?"

41

"I think Pat means the ark, not the Arctic," muttered Einstein. "I'm not saying that Pat is stupid, but if he had a pet zebra, he'd call it Spot."

Rolling her eyes, Ms. Warren said, "Chloe, can you answer the question?"

"Antarctica is the icy continent at the bottom of the world," said Chloe. "Everyone knows that."

Einstein raised his hand, and Ms. Warren called on him. "Antarctica is not actually the bottom of the world," he said. "It depends which way you turn the globe. There's no reason to call the north top and the south bottom when you talk about our planet in space. It could easily be the other way. In fact—"

"That's enough, Einstein," said Ms. Warren. "This is not a science class. This is a social studies class. And we are learning about an explorer who went to Antarctica. I don't think that science has anything to do with his journals."

"Science has to do with nearly everything, Ms. Warren," said Einstein. "I was reading—"

"Enough!" said Ms. Warren. Her face was getting as red as a tomato. "Let's get on with reading the journal."

"Yeah, shut up, Einstein," said Pat. "Herman and I want to learn about the Arctic or whatever."

"Now, let me think about that," said Joel, another student in the class. "I can't believe what I heard. You want to learn something, Pat? If you suddenly got amnesia, you would know more than you do now."

"That's enough talking!" exclaimed Ms. Warren. "I'm going to read one of the entries in Helmut Jorgansen's journal. And I want all of you to be quiet and listen carefully. We can learn how difficult life was for one of the early explorers of Antarctica."

Ms. Warren opened the journal and began to read from a page that she had marked.

"I arrived at the Ross Ice Shelf in January of 1853, which is the beginning of the summer in the Southern Hemisphere. No one has been here before us except for James Clark Ross, in 1841, and the continent has never been explored.

"We anchored our sailing ship offshore at the edge of the ice sheet that covered the ocean waters. I dropped down onto the ice

43

and began to walk toward the shore. The ice was a yard thick. But no sooner had I begun to walk than the ice suddenly heaved up around me, and two killer whales burst forth from underneath. One was only a few yards away. Its black-and-white head rose out of the water, and the killer peered at me. Its mouth opened and displayed a fearsome array of teeth. I saw a cloud of vapor spew out of its nostrils as it snorted and blew. I thought how very unpleasant it would be to lose my life before I had even begun to explore the continent. Fortunately, the killer whales swam away, and I was able to continue walking.

"The ice sheet and the icebergs were beautiful. I saw one iceberg that was emerald green, just like in the Coleridge poem 'The Rime of the Ancient Mariner': 'And ice, mast-high, came floating by/As green as Emerald.'

"Closer to shore I came upon huge flocks of emperor penguins. I also saw some of the animals that prey upon them: the leopard seal, the skua bird, and the great white polar bear. It is amazing how so many of the emperors and other penguins manage to survive the attacks of these fearsome beasts.

"Too soon, I decided to go back to the ship and gather supplies. Tomorrow, I and two of my shipmates will start our trek to reach the South Pole. It will be an unbelievable journey."

"And I don't believe it," said Einstein without waiting to be called on.

"Why not?" asked Ms. Warren.

"Because there is one very bad mistake in Jorgansen's journal," replied Einstein. "And if he made that big a mistake, I doubt if he had ever seen the continent for himself. He was just relying on the knowledge of Antarctica people had over a hundred years ago. He must have been describing what he had read in some other book, and it's just wrong scientifically."

Can you solve the mystery: What bad mistake did Jorgansen make in his story?

"Well, maybe Jorgansen did take some liberties in describing the emerald green of an iceberg. We all know that icebergs are white. Still, he was just being poetic. We call it poetic license," said Ms. Warren.

"That's not it," objected Einstein. "One out of a thousand icebergs *is* green. Most icebergs look bluish white. Ice looks blue because of the way it reflects light. But a few bergs have yellow in them from dead plankton plants trapped in the ice. Yellow plus blue equals green. So some icebergs look green."

"Then what is it?" asked Ms. Warren. "And how can you be so sure he is not telling the truth about everything else?"

"Because of what he said about the animals that prey on penguins. The description of the killer whales is accurate as far as it goes, though it's very unlikely that they would have attacked a person. And leopard seals and skuas hunt penguins, too. But Jorgansen couldn't possibly have seen a polar bear, because there are no polar bears in the Antarctic. Polar bears live twelve thousand miles away, in the Arctic."

46

"Yeah, I knew that," said Pat. "I told you that it was in the ark. Polar bears live in the arky place, whatever you said. See, I told you that before Einstein. I'm the best thinker in the whole class."

Einstein shook his head. "Pat," he said, "you're the best at all you do. And since all you do is brag, that's the only thing you're good at."

6

The Case of the

SHINING BLUE PLANET

"i think this is my breakthrough science discovery, Einstein," Stanley Roberts said. The teenage science buff impatiently pushed back his long black hair, which was forever falling over his eyes. "I know this is the New Year's weekend, but I'm glad you came over to my laboratory. Now take a look at my computer. I just found this incredible website. You won't believe the opportunities to make science explorations that I found on the Internet."

"You mean like the backward space alien,"

48

Einstein said innocently. He liked the older boy but enjoyed kidding him. "Or the photograph of the biggest animal ever seen? You thought those people were going to send you a dinosaur photograph taken by a time machine. And when you paid them twenty-five dollars, they sent you a photo of a blue whale, which really is the biggest animal that ever lived."

"Never mind about that," said Stanley impatiently. "Those are small failures in the life of a scientist. This will be a great success. I'm sure of it!"

Einstein walked slowly through Stanley's "laboratory." The attic room was overflowing with electronic gear, computers, a humanoid figure that looked like a half-finished robot, plastic containers, rocks and minerals, and all kinds of test tubes and beakers. It was even more cluttered than the last time Einstein was there.

"Stanley," Einstein said, "I think you should remember that if at first you don't succeed, try reading the directions."

"Is that so, Einstein?" Stanley said. "Then

just tell me what you think about this. Look at the photograph on the computer monitor."

Einstein looked at the screen. It showed a picture of a beautiful blue-and-white globe. Einstein knew that it was a photo of Earth taken from space. He knew that the blue and white were caused by Earth's atmosphere, its clouds, and its oceans. Underneath the photo was a caption that said the picture had been taken recently from a space satellite by astronauts as their spacecraft orbited Earth.

"This website is all about sending up a space satellite for communications and research," said Stanley. "The person in charge of the project was a cosmonaut from the former Soviet Union. His name is Dr. Kronkheit. He told me that he and several other cosmonauts had never been publicized because they had been doing spy research."

"I thought spies buy their equipment at a snoopermarket," said Einstein. "What does Dr. Kronkheit want you to do?"

Stanley disregarded Einstein's joke. "Dr. K. wants me to send him fifty dollars. That money enrolls me in the satellite program and allows me to perform one experiment in space. For every additional fifty dollars, I can perform one more experiment. Would you like to join, too?"

"It sounds very strange to me," said Einstein. "Sending up a space satellite costs a lot of money."

"That's what I thought, too," replied Stanley. "But Dr. K. sent me a lot of detailed pages of mathematical formulas that explain how he can send up a satellite for a lot less money than you think."

"Do you understand the formulas?" asked Einstein.

"No," admitted Stanley. "But just read Dr. K.'s description of blasting off from Earth. Here it is on his website. Let me go to that link."

Stanley used his computer mouse to move a pointer over a blue line at the bottom of the page that read: *Click here for a description of Kronkheit's first space launch.* Stanley clicked twice with the button on his mouse, and a page of text appeared on the screen. "Read this," Stanley said.

Einstein looked at the screen and began to read:

Starting in the 1950s, experimental rocket planes have taken photographs of Earth from the edge of space. But the most spectacular photographs of our shining blue-and-white planet have been taken by the spaceships that the Soviet Union and the United States sent

into space from the 1960s until the present day.

No one who has ever been in a spaceship will ever be able to forget the thrill of first seeing our planet from space. I'll never forget my first liftoff in a rocket ship in the early 1960s. It was a winter day, with blue skies and white clouds. When the rocket ship blasted off, we passed quickly through the clouds and could see their tops below us. The altimeter read one hundred miles, and we were going up fast. All around us the blue sky spread out as far as you could see. Above us, the moon and the stars twinkled in the blue. It was the most beautiful sight I have ever seen.

Einstein pushed back his glasses, which were slipping off the end of his nose. "I don't think the so-called Dr. Kronkheit has ever been a cosmonaut," he said. "And I wouldn't send him any money if I were you, Stanley," he added.

Can you solve the mystery: What made Einstein realize that Dr. Kronkheit was a phony cosmonaut?

53

"Why?" asked Stanley. "The Earth does look blue and white from space."

"Our planet does look like a blue globe from space," Einstein agreed. "But it's surrounded by darkness. The blue sky, the white clouds, and most of the other colors we see in the sky come from light being reflected in different directions when the light collides with air and water molecules. But as you go higher than twelve miles above the surface, the sky begins turning dark around you, because there are fewer molecules of air and water."

"But the Earth still looks blue and white from space," said Stanley.

"Yes," said Einstein. "If you look down from a spaceship, the planet still looks blue and white. But darkness is all around you, and the moon and the stars are set against a black sky, not a blue one."

"Oh," said Stanley dejectedly. "I guess I shouldn't listen to so-called experts without making sure of their facts."

"Yeah," said Einstein. "It reminds me of the weather forecaster who assured Noah before the Flood that it was only going to be a light drizzle."

7

The Case of the

ELECTRIFYING COWS

very so often Einstein's father would take one of his sons to his office when there was no school. Today was a school holiday, and Dr. Anderson had asked Einstein if he would like to come to his veterinary office. Einstein enjoyed watching his dad at work, so he agreed promptly.

Dr. Anderson was kind and gentle as he examined his patients. He usually found out what was wrong quickly without upsetting the animal or its owner. He often would treat stray cats and dogs that children had found injured or needing some medical attention. He would fix them up, give them shots, and keep them at his clinic until he found a place for them to stay. Some of the animals had been there for years. Dr. Anderson had the reputation for being the best and nicest veterinarian in the county.

All morning long, a procession of dogs, cats, and other small pets were brought in to be examined. Einstein's job was to get each animal's records from the computer files. Einstein knew many of the animals from other visits, and he would pet them and play with them whenever he had the chance. He also helped by holding the animals while his father examined them.

To help calm down the owners and their pets, Einstein kept up a running patter of jokes about the animals he was holding. He asked one dog owner, "Did you hear about the man who had trouble with his watchdog? The trouble was, all the dog watched was TV."

The man smiled and groaned.

"I once heard about a dog that was so

smart, its owner taught it how to play chess," added Einstein.

"A dog that plays chess? That's incredible!" said the man.

"Not really. The owner beat it two out of three times."

Dr. Anderson's next patient was a cat. As he was holding the animal to keep it from squirming, Einstein asked the owner, "Do you know the names of four members of the cat family?"

"You mean like lions and tigers?" asked the owner.

"The father cat, the mother cat, and two kittens," said Einstein. "I knew a cat that was so intelligent, if you asked it how much was two minus two, it said nothing," he continued.

At that joke both the owner and Dr. Anderson groaned.

At one point Dr. Anderson examined a parrot that kept repeating, "Polly wants a cracker. Polly wants a cracker."

"Not much of a conversation," said Einstein. "Dad, did you hear what the parrot said after it laid a square egg?"

"What did it say?" responded Dr. Anderson with a smile.

"Ouch!" replied Einstein.

Dr. Anderson shook his head and rolled his eyes.

Later that morning, after the rush was over, Dr. Anderson said to his son, "I've been trying to find someone to help with the animals in the clinic. I've advertised the position, and job applications have come in from people all over the county. One of the résumés is from someone named Alex Wolfe. It's pretty impressive. I'd like you to read it over and tell me what you think. Wolfe is coming in for an interview shortly before lunch."

Dr. Anderson paused and then smiled. "Wolfe is a good name for an animal helper, don't you think?"

"It sure is," agreed Einstein. Wolves were one of his favorite animals. "Do you know when wolves have thirty-two feet?" he asked his father.

"When they are in a pack of eight," responded his father. "You already told me that joke, Einstein."

Einstein grinned sheepishly and took the job application to the desk in the waiting room. The top sheet was a summary of Alex Wolfe's training and job experiences. According to the application, Wolfe had a college degree with a major in animal studies, a year of employment at a store called PetWorld, a year working on a cattle ranch in Texas, and another year working as an animal trainer for a circus in Florida. He also had letters of reference from several people, including the director of the circus, who called Wolfe "an intelligent young man with a wonderful imagination about animals."

Wolfe had also written an essay to help him get the job. The title of the essay was "A Proposal to Train Cows Using Pavlov's Conditioning Methods."

In the essay, Wolfe explained how he wanted to use conditioning to teach cows to respond to all kinds of commands. He quoted from previous experiments:

When Pavlov trained dogs, he rang a bell and then gave them food to eat. After a while, the dogs would salivate whenever Pavlov rang the bell even if there was no food to be seen. We call that kind of behavior a conditioned reflex. I propose to teach cows by the same method.

Wolfe went on to suggest that cows could be trained to stand up and lie down by means of a mild electric shock. He proposed blowing a whistle once while giving the cows a mild electric shock on their backs to make them lie down. Then he would blow a whistle twice and give the cows a mild electric shock on their throats to make them stand up. Wolfe's essay continued:

An electric shock to a cow's throat will stimulate its front legs to move. The front legs will go up and then the hind legs have to follow. You can do this with groups of cows and make them all stand up or sit down at once. Can you imagine how wonderful it would be to have a herd of trained cows? After they've been trained properly, you could make them go into the barn and get into their milking stalls just by blowing a whistle.

Wolfe's application went on for several more pages, suggesting how people could use conditioning on animal farms across the country. Einstein had just finished reading the application when a man came into the clinic.

"I'm Alex Wolfe," the man said, introducing himself. "I have an appointment to see Dr. Anderson."

"Please have a seat," said Einstein. "I'll tell my father you're here."

Einstein went into Dr. Anderson's office and put the application on his father's desk. When he told his father that Mr. Wolfe was in the waiting room, his father asked, "What do you think of Wolfe's application? How about those electrified cows?"

"I don't think that Wolfe has nearly as much experience with animals as he says he does," responded Einstein, "even if he does know how Pavlov trained dogs."

"You're right, Einstein," said Dr. Anderson.

"Wolfe probably made up some of his work experiences. But he does have a great imagination. And I like his eagerness. But what did you notice that was wrong about his application?"

Can you solve the mystery: What makes Einstein think that Wolfe is making up some of his job training?

"Anyone who has ever seen cattle knows that they get up from a lying position with their back end first," said Einstein. "So touching their *throats* with a mild electric shock would not do much good. It would be better to touch their rear ends with a shock to make them move."

"That's right," agreed Dr. Anderson. "Wolfe said he worked on a cattle farm for a year, yet he doesn't seem to know that."

"I wonder if Wolfe knows why cows wear bells," mused Einstein.

"O.K.," said Dr. Anderson. "Tell me why cows wear bells."

"Because their horns don't work," responded Einstein.

"I think you should put that joke out to pasture," said Dr. Anderson with a shake of his head. "Send in Mr. Wolfe, and after the interview I'll take you out to lunch."

"Dad, do you know what's the best thing to put in an ice-cream soda?" asked Einstein. "A straw."

Dr. Anderson groaned and held his nose to indicate what he thought of the joke.

8

The Case of the

DiSAPPEARiNG SNoWBALL

The first Tuesday in February was Winter Carnival at Sparta Middle School. It had snowed heavily the week before, and snowdrifts still covered the ground. When Tuesday arrived, the sun was shining, but it was quite cold and windy.

School buses were lined up to take all the students to Big Lake State Park. It had an indoor ice-skating rink and field house, and there were ski slopes and plenty of space for other activities.

As Einstein's sixth-grade class boarded its

bus, the boys and girls began to cheer and clap. Despite the cold, everyone was looking forward to the carnival.

Winter Carnival was a always a fun day. There would be sled and ski races, ice hockey, speed and figure skating, and many other winter games for the sixth, seventh, and eighth grades. There would also be silly contests, such as a weird-snow-statue competition, a slipping-on-ice meet, and a snowball-melting contest. At lunchtime, everyone was to go into the park's field house for hot soup and sandwiches.

To liven things up during lunch, each class had set up an indoor booth for games. Einstein's class made a baseball-throwing booth. In the booth, one of the students in the class would put on an old laboratory coat to protect his or her clothing and then balance on a swing right over a cream pie. For a small donation to the school book fund, contestants got to throw three balls. If one of the balls hit a board attached to the swing, the person would fall off, onto the pie.

Pat wouldn't let the class vote on who got to sit on the swing. He knew that either he or

Herman would have been elected. So the class decided that, instead, the person who lost the snowball-melting contest would have to sit on the swing.

"I hope you came up with some idea of how to make Pat lose the snowball-melting competition," Margaret said to Einstein as their bus pulled away from the school. "Know any scientific research on how to make snowballs last longer?"

"I don't know if snowballs are high on anyone's research list," admitted Einstein as he pushed up his glasses. "But do you know why snow is like a tree?"

"No," said Margaret, "but I'm sure I'm going to find out in a minute."

"Because it *leaves* in the spring."

"Einstein!" exclaimed Margaret. "Enough jokes. Let's concentrate on figuring out how we can use science to make sure that Pat loses the snowball-melting contest."

"It isn't going to be easy," said Einstein. "The class is split into two-person teams. Every team is supposed to make a snowball that is as big as a basketball. Then we each leave our snowball in a shed until lunchtime.

The team with the smallest snowball is the one that has to sit in the booth."

"The problem," said Margaret, "is making sure that Pat's snowball melts faster than any of the others. One way to do that is to get his to melt. The other way is make the others last longer. Is there any way we can make sure that all the other snowballs last longer?"

"Not that I can think of," said Einstein, "because no team is supposed to do anything to its snowball other than make it with snow. Of course, since Pat always cheats, maybe I can get him to cheat in the wrong way."

Einstein thought for a moment. "That's an idea," he said. "If Pat cheats and loses, then it's not our fault. And I think I know what we can try to do. Let's change our seats. I want to get near enough to Pat and Herman so that they can hear us talking. Just make sure to play along with what I say."

Einstein and Margaret got up and made their way to the empty seats around Pat and Herman. There were plenty to choose from, because the two boys had been throwing spitballs at the other students when the teacher wasn't looking.

"It's too bad that we can't use iron in the snowballs," Einstein said to Margaret in a loud voice as they sat down in front of Pat and Herman. Einstein could see that the two of them had become quiet and seemed to be straining their ears to hear what he was saying.

"Why is that?" asked Margaret in an equally loud voice. "What good would iron do?"

"Well, iron is an excellent conductor of heat," Einstein said. "And you know that conducting heat away from snow would keep it from melting."

Margaret looked at Einstein and nodded her head. "Oh, of course," she responded. "Now why didn't I think of that? But where could we get some iron?"

"Well, I certainly wouldn't think of cheating," said Einstein. "But I do have iron filings in our bag for the science magic show we're going to put on during lunch. Now, if I were a cheater, I might take those iron filings and..." His voice trailed off. "I just realized that someone may be listening to us," he continued. "Let's go back to our other seats."

As soon as Einstein and Margaret left, Pat began to whisper to Herman. "Now we got 'em!" he exclaimed, punching Herman on the arm and laughing.

"What was all that about?" asked Margaret. "I know that iron is a good conductor of heat, but what does that have to do with letting Pat and Herman hear what you said?"

"Pat and Herman will cheat any chance they get," replied Einstein. "And I wanted to make sure that they knew they could get some iron filings from our bag of props for the science magic show. I think that they'll try to cheat by mixing the iron filings with their snowball."

"But what good is that going to do, since the iron filings will be mixed in with the snow?" asked Margaret.

"Just wait and see," answered Einstein with a grin. "Pat and Herman don't just act stupid. With them, it's the real thing."

When Einstein's class arrived at Big Lake State Park, all the kids started to work at packing their snowballs. Einstein noticed that Pat and Herman went back into the bus and came out whispering to each other before they made their snowball.

When all the snowballs were made and lined up inside an equipment shed, the shed was locked so that no one could see what was happening to the snowballs until later that day.

The rest of the morning was spent on the outdoor snow contests. Einstein's class won the weird-snow-statue contest. They had built a huge spaceship out of ice and snow. The spaceship seemed to have landed, and a door at the bottom was open. In front of the door was a funny-looking alien who appeared to be trying to communicate with a dog sitting in front of him. The alien was holding a sign that read: Take me to your leader. The dog wasn't paying any attention to the sign. He just had his head cocked to one side, as if he were waiting for a dog biscuit.

The idea of the slipping-on-ice contest was for someone to take a run and then begin sliding on the ice just at the starting line. The person who slid the longest was the winner. Some contestants started to slide too soon and didn't go very far. Others began their slide beyond the starting line and were disqualified. Pat and Herman both entered the contest. Herman tripped and slid past the starting line before he crashed into a snowbank. Pat tried to start sliding several feet beyond the line and complained loudly when he was disqualified. The contest was finally declared a draw between two people in Einstein's class, Benjamin and Chloe.

When it was almost lunchtime, the class assembled in front of the equipment shed, and the door was unlocked by their science teacher, Ms. Taylor.

Everyone burst out laughing when they saw what had happened. Everyone except Pat and Herman. All the other kids' snowballs were pretty much alike in size, but Pat and Herman's had melted away to practically nothing.

"It looks like Pat and Herman are going to

take turns sitting in pie," announced Ms. Taylor. "Their snowball is clearly the loser in the contest."

"I told you never to listen to Einstein," Pat said to Herman angrily. He punched him on the arm.

"Huh?" said Herman. "I didn't listen to Einstein! You were the one who told me to get the iron filings and mix them with the snow."

"Never mind," growled Pat. "Herman, you're just going to have to get ready to sit in pie." He glared at Einstein and walked away.

"O.K.," said Margaret. "So you were responsible for Pat's snowball melting so quickly. Now explain how you knew."

"I knew that Pat would listen to me and try to cheat," explained Einstein. "And I figured that he would think that mixing iron filings with snow would conduct heat away from the snow. But that's not what happens at all."

Can you solve the mystery: What did Einstein know was going to happen when Pat and Herman mixed iron filings with the snow?

"So what did happen?" Margaret asked.

"When Pat mixed the iron filings with the snow, the iron started to combine with oxygen in the air and began to rust," explained Einstein. "As iron rusts, it gives off heat. The heat melted Pat and Herman's snowball faster than anyone else's."

"I see," said Margaret. "Say, that's not a bad idea for keeping your hands warm on a cold winter day. Just keep them next to rusting iron."

"It's already been done," said Einstein. "Some ski manufacturers are putting small amounts of iron powder into a sealed packet. When the packet is opened, it gives off enough heat to keep a skier's hands warm for a couple of hours."

"That will teach Pat to cheat," Margaret said.

9

The Case of the

CREATURE FROM BENEATH THE ICE

T he Winter Carnival at Big Lake State Park was going well. The day was sunny but very cold and getting colder. The cold didn't bother the students of Sparta Middle School, though. Most of them were engaged in winter sports, from ice-skating to snowball throwing. The day had been a lot of fun for everyone. Everyone, that is, except Pat and Herman. They had lost the snowball-melting contest and, as a result, had been reluctant targets in the class baseball-throwing booth during lunch. After lunch, the two of them had walked off, muttering that they would get even with everybody.

Einstein was talking to his friends Margaret, Joel, Benjamin, and Chloe. "Pat and Herman have no real enemies in the class," he observed, "just lots of friends who don't like them."

"Kids try to be nice to Pat, but he's his own worst enemy," said Joel.

"Not while I'm around," said Benjamin with a laugh. Benjamin and Joel were as big and strong as Pat and Herman.

"I feel sorry for Herman," said Chloe. "He doesn't even seem to mind that Pat is always blaming him for everything. Herman is the perfect fall guy for Pat's mistakes. He never complains about anything that Pat does to him."

"Pat is the kind of friend who's always around when he needs someone," said Margaret. "But let's forget about those two. We have the rest of the afternoon free. Einstein and I are going to hike up to High Point and take photographs from the peak. What are you three going to do?"

"We're going ice-skating on Big Lake," responded Chloe. "I just got a new pair of figure skates."

"Benjamin and I have speed skates," explained Joel, "but we'll hang around Chloe just in case Pat and Herman come over and begin pestering her. They're always trying to impress her by teasing her. But they'll think twice when they see us there."

"Right," said Benjamin. "I'd like to see them try to get physical with us. They'd be sorry."

As Einstein and Margaret walked up the hill to High Point, Einstein spotted some animal tracks in the snow. They led from a hole in the ground into a nearby thicket of bushes. Einstein bent down and examined the tracks. "These footprints were made by a cottontail rabbit," he said. "The hole was probably made by a woodchuck, and the rabbit may have used the woodchuck burrow for shelter."

"The woodchuck is probably hibernating," said Margaret. "Too bad for him. I would hate to hibernate during winter. I love the way the

77

trees look against the snow. See the silvery branches and dark trunks of those red maples? And look at the twisty branches of the cherry trees. When the leaves are down, you can see the framework of each tree."

Einstein and Margaret walked on in silence. Every so often, one would point out some interesting winter sight to the other. As they went, they spotted a gray squirrel sitting on a tree limb, heard a loud cawing from several large black crows, and watched a field full of red-winged blackbirds.

They took photographs along the way and at the top of the peak. From the highest point, they could see small farmhouses, red barns, and long fields that were now covered by snow. Off in the far distance, over the hills, was a line of small mountains, covered with ice. The day was so clear that they could see for many miles.

It was only three in the afternoon, but the sun was already sinking toward the horizon as they walked back in the direction of the frozen lake.

"Isn't it interesting that the shortest day of the year is the *first* day of winter, the winter solstice," Einstein said. "Each day after that, the hours of daylight grow longer until the first day of summer, the summer solstice. So as soon as winter or summer begins, it starts to end."

As Einstein and Margaret got nearer to the lake, they spotted Joel, Benjamin, and Chloe running toward them. Their friends seemed to be very agitated.

"I wonder what's wrong," Margaret said to Einstein. "I hope that Pat and Herman haven't been bothering them."

"What happened?" asked Einstein as their friends came up to them. "Did Pat try to pull some trick on you?"

"I'm not sure," said Chloe. "While we were skating, we began to hear some strange noises. They seemed to come from beneath the ice on the lake. At first, I thought that it was just Pat and Herman trying to scare us. But now I'm not so sure. How could they have made noises that seemed to be coming from underneath the ice?"

"What did the noises sound like?" asked Margaret.

"I've never heard anything like them

before," said Benjamin. "At first they sounded like squeaking or growling. Then they sounded like a sharp crack and a rumble right afterward. You think it might be some kind of creature that lives under the ice?"

"Maybe it's the Abominable Snowman," said Joel. "Maybe he lives down there and wakes up when the sun goes down. Or maybe it's just Pat and Herman making those strange noises. I think we'd better stay off the ice until we find out what it is."

"There are Pat and Herman now," said Margaret. "They're running over here. Let's see what they have to say."

Pat and Herman arrived panting and out of breath. "Did you hear those noises?" asked Pat. "Herman and me were walking by the lake, and we heard these rumbling sounds. Herman thinks it came from under the ice. Einstein, what do you think? Are those noises being made by some kind of monster that lives beneath the ice?"

"Pat, I bet that you and Herman made those noises to scare us," said Chloe. "You're always trying to scare people."

"No way!" said Pat. "We didn't do a thing. Did we, Herman? You tell 'em!"

"Huh?" said Herman. "It wasn't Pat. He said he was scared of the noise."

"Shut up, Herman!" ordered Pat. "What do *you* think it is, Einstein?"

"If you know what it is, Einstein, please tell us," said Chloe.

Einstein pushed back his glasses, which were slipping down. "I think I know what made those noises," he said.

Can you solve the mystery: Did Pat and Herman make those weird noises, or is there a creature living beneath the ice of the lake?

"Tell me again exactly what the noises sounded like," Einstein said.

"Like sharp cracking sounds," said Chloe.

"And a rumble," added Benjamin.

"It almost sounded as if something was talking to us," said Joel.

"Yeah, it was a cracking, rumbling, talking sound," said Pat.

"Huh?" said Herman.

"From your descriptions, I don't think that Pat and Herman had anything to do with those sounds," said Einstein.

"See! What did I tell you?" exclaimed Pat. "I never did anything."

"So if it wasn't them, who did make the sounds, Einstein?" asked Joel.

"I've heard those kinds of sounds before when this lake is frozen. I think that the noises are made by the ice," Einstein explained.

"That's silly," said Pat. "Ice can't talk."

"It can't talk, but it can and does make noises. Water expands when it freezes and becomes ice. That's why ice floats: The volume has increased, but the weight remains

82

the same. So the original volume must weigh less. It's now lighter than the water underneath. When the freezing water expands, it squeezes outward in all directions. And as the ice thaws in the sun and then freezes again as the sun goes down, it pushes and shoves against itself. That makes it crack and rumble."

"So there isn't any creature beneath the ice," said Chloe. "I guess we can all go back and skate some more on Big Lake."

"What did I tell you, Herman," said Pat. "That's exactly what I said. The ice was talking, I said. See, Herman, you're just stupid."

"But, Pat," Herman said, "you told me to run. You said you were scared. I just ran like you told me. And I'm not stupid," he added. "I've got more brains in my little finger than I have in my whole head."

"I've got more stuff in my head than you do, Herman," shouted Pat.

"Pat, your head is worth more than diamonds," said Einstein. "Or at least it's harder."

10

The Case of the

HYPNOTIZED FROG

instein and Margaret had decided to go on a science collecting trip one Saturday in early spring. It had been a rainy week, but Saturday was sunny. The air was crisp, and the temperature was pleasant. A gentle wind blew a few white puffy clouds across the blue sky.

"Those are cumulus clouds," said Margaret. "I love to see the way their shape changes as they move. Right now they look like balls of cotton, don't they? When they get raggedy in the wind, they're called fractocumulus. *Fracto* means 'broken.'"

"Those clouds are beautiful," agreed Einstein. "They look like sheep grazing in the sky." He shifted the weight of his backpack so it was more comfortable. "When are we going to have our picnic lunch?" he asked.

"Einstein, you're always hungry," replied Margaret with a laugh. "We just had breakfast at my house a little while ago."

"But I had practically nothing to eat," he complained. "You kept hurrying me to finish."

"Nothing to eat! Are you serious? You had orange juice, cereal and milk, scrambled eggs, and two slices of toast and jam. My mother couldn't believe all the food you were piling in."

"Yeah, your mom really makes great eggs. But I wish you would stop talking about food. You're just making me hungrier." Einstein grinned. "I think I'll show your mother how to serve dinosaur eggs," he said. "With hot mastodon."

Margaret struggled to hide her smile. "Arrggghh," she said. "Here come the egg jokes."

"You know how many eggs I can eat on an empty stomach?" asked Einstein.

"Twenty or thirty?"

"Nah," said Einstein. "Only one, because then my stomach won't be empty."

"Einstein!" said Margaret warningly.

"O.K., no more egg jokes," agreed Einstein. "I know when I'm beaten." He paused. "Beaten, get it?"

"I got it, but I hope it isn't catching," said Margaret. "Now let's concentrate on what we're supposed to be doing today. We're setting up a natural pond aquarium in class, and we have to collect some water plants and pond water."

"Yeah," said Einstein. "I'd also like to find two or three tadpoles to add to the aquarium, so we can observe the way they behave. We can keep them in the aquarium, and when they change into frogs, we can bring them back to the pond and release them."

"Good idea," agreed Margaret. "Anything we collect in nature, we should return to nature."

"You know what the mean kid said to the frog?" asked Einstein. "'I hope you croak.'"

"Arrggghh," said Margaret again.

"When frogs need to have their eyes examined, they go to a hoptician," continued Einstein.

"Bad!" said Margaret. "One more frog joke and no lunch."

"Jug-a-rumph," replied Einstein. But he was quiet after that.

Einstein and Margaret followed a winding trail that led down through trees and meadows to Beaver Pond. The ground was soggy with rain and melted snow. Small temporary streams flowed down the hillside. Some of the rivulets formed spring pools behind dams of twigs and dead leaves.

Einstein stopped and pointed to the ground. "Look at the worm castings along the ground," he said. "And look at the tiny dark spiders running over the leaves. That tunnel opening over there? Probably made by a mole."

"I love the way the pussy willows look in the spring," said Margaret. "When they first appeared, they were silver. But now they look golden." She paused to run her fingers over the furry catkins of the pussy willow trees.

When they got to the pond, Margaret pointed excitedly at a movement in the water. "It's a baby painted turtle," she said. "It's so *small*," she added. "Only about the size of my palm." The turtle swam slowly among the clouds of algae in the pond. Its red and black colors were sharp and shiny.

Margaret and Einstein were quiet as they watched the turtle swim. In the distance, they could hear the sound of a woodpecker drumming against a tree and the croak of a frog from across the water. One side of the pond was filled with green sword leaves and the upright stalks of cattails. Each stalk carried two closely packed clumps of tiny flowers. To Einstein, the lower clump looked like a greenish brown sausage. Even though his stomach was growling, he decided not to mention that to Margaret.

"Look at the leopard frogs," Einstein whispered, gesturing to the edge of the pond. The frogs were sitting half-submerged along the edges. They were green and had darker spots ringed with white. Every so often, one would inflate its throat and croak, a low, hoarse *ker-r-r-ock, ker-r-r-ock.* One frog suddenly jumped into the water. It looked streamlined and speedy, and its pure white belly flashed in the sun.

"Aren't they beautiful?" Margaret asked.

"Here's an earthworm," said Einstein. "Would you mind if I fed it to one of the frogs?"

Margaret looked at the earthworm. She loved animals, even earthworms, and was always unhappy when she fed one animal to another, even though she knew it happened in nature all the time.

"I'll do it," she said unenthusiastically. "You go around to the other side of the pond and see if you can collect a few tadpoles while I feed your earthworm to a frog."

"Sure," Einstein agreed. He respected Margaret's attitude about animals and never made fun of her feelings.

"My, this earthworm is wriggling," said Margaret thoughtfully. "I bet it would like to go back into the soil."

Einstein didn't reply. He walked around the pond and was able to capture a half dozen tiny tadpoles. He placed them in a large plastic bag along with a supply of pond water and some green algae.

When he got back to the other side of the pond, Margaret was smiling. "Guess what?" she said. "I wriggled that earthworm in front of a frog, and it suddenly snapped up the worm with its tongue. It happened so fast, you could hardly see it. And all the time that old frog looked straight at me. It ate that

earthworm and never even blinked its eyes once. It looked as if it was hypnotized."

Einstein smiled. "That frog may have been hypnotized, but I'm not. You never fed that earthworm to a frog."

"Come on, Einstein," said Margaret. "How do you know that? You couldn't see what I was doing from the other side of the pond."

"No," admitted Einstein. "But your story about feeding the earthworm to the frog just doesn't *hop* true."

Can you solve the mystery: How does Einstein know that Margaret made up the story about the frog eating the earthworm?

Margaret smiled. "So I let the earthworm go. Big deal! But how did you know?"

"I guessed that you must have let it go because of the way you said the frog was eating the worm," said Einstein. "I knew when you described the frog as never shutting its eyes the whole time and being hypnotized while it ate the worm."

"So? Frogs stare without blinking."

"Not while they're eating," said Einstein. "Those big, beautiful bulging frog eyes have to shut while the frog eats. The underside of a frog's eyes bulge down into its mouth. By shutting its eyes, a frog pushes the food down into its stomach. Frogs use their eyeballs when they eat in the same way that we use our tongues when we eat."

"Guess I shouldn't have tried to fool you," said Margaret contritely.

"That's O.K.," said Einstein. "I understand how you feel about feeding one animal to another." Einstein rubbed his stomach. "But all this talk about food and feeding is making me hungry," he said. "And as you know, food is an essential part of my balanced diet."

Margaret grinned. "Let's eat," she said.